Ba Big Blue Vacation

by Marley Hayes
illustrated by Christiane Beauregard

Harcourt
SCHOOL PUBLISHERS

Printed in China

ISBN 10: 0-15-350989-9
ISBN 13: 978-0-15-350989-6

Ordering Options
ISBN 10: 0-15-350601-6 (Grade 4 On-Level Collection)
ISBN 13: 978-0-15-350601-7 (Grade 4 On-Level Collection)
ISBN 10: 0-15-357942-0 (package of 5)
ISBN 13: 978-0-15-357942-4 (package of 5)

2 3 4 5 6 7 8 9 10 985 12 11 10 09 08 07

BOOM! The sound echoed around Babe the Blue Ox as he pulled the colossal tree out of the forest. It was as big a tree as anyone could imagine, with a trunk thicker and wider than the trains that rolled across the Midwest. The huge ox, though, pulled it as easily as if it were a toothpick.

Paul Bunyan grinned and waved at Babe. Then Paul tossed the tree onto the pile of other trees they had brought out of the forest that day.

"Well, that's it for the day," said Paul. "You know, Babe, I've been thinking about going on a vacation."

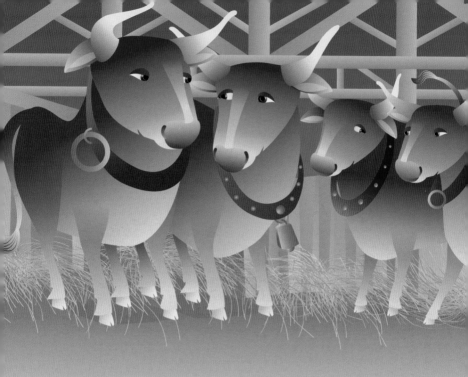

"That sounds like a mighty fine idea," said Babe cordially.

Paul gave a hearty laugh. "Well, of course, that means you get a vacation, too."

Babe went home that night and explained the situation to his wife, Bessie, their son, Blue, and daughter, Belle. They all agreed that it was an exciting opportunity to get out and see new places and do new things. Blue wanted to go find some mountains and climb on top of them. Belle thought she would like to go to the beach and maybe swim across an ocean or two.

4

Bessie had the best suggestion—why not go on a scenic tour of the country and see mountains, beaches, and more? A few weeks later, the oxen packed up, waved good-bye to the Bunyans, and set off at dawn.

They didn't have to go far before they reached their first destination, the Great Lakes. The family stopped off at each of the *six* lakes to splash around and play. When they got to the last lake, they were all pretty thirsty, so they drank and drank and drank until the whole lake was empty. That's why today there are only five Great Lakes.

The oxen decided to head east and visit New York City. The city's tall buildings were just the right height for the oxen to lean against and take a rest every now and then. There were also plenty of people on the streets. People would look up and stare at the gigantic blue oxen, but then they would just shake their heads as if they had seen an illusion and go about their busy ways. City people were in too much of a hurry to worry about such fanciful things as big blue oxen visiting from Minnesota.

Babe and his family were hefty oxen, and the steps they took left holes in the ground. The city officials looked at these big holes and worried about filling them. Then someone had the idea to use the holes to build tunnels and run trains underground. That would make the streets less crowded and help the busy people get to places even faster.

Everyone agreed that it was a superb idea, and that's how the New York City subway system was born. The family decided they were ready for some warmth, so they turned south.

In Florida, it was so hot that it felt like the sun had come down from the sky and was sitting on the beach. The palm trees were busy fanning each other, and many fish decided to swim north to cool off from the heat.

Blue and Belle loved to play in the waves. To be honest, they could be a little rough sometimes. One day, they were splashing around with so much energy that the waves that were coming toward the shore were turned around right back toward the ocean. As they went back out to sea, the waves became bigger and bigger.

There was a huge hurricane coming, but the big waves knocked it down and broke it into small rain showers. Blue and Belle had done Florida a favor without even realizing it!

Bessie said she had heard that there were plenty of cattle in Texas, and she thought that would be a nice place to visit. However, a terrible drought had been going on there. Fortunately, one of Babe's horns hooked on to a big rain cloud while they were walking from Florida, and he dragged it with him all the way to Texas. It burst open, and everyone in Texas enjoyed a nice cool downpour.

One day, the oxen were taking a leisurely
walk through Kansas when they noticed that
the tiny little people below them were running
and looking very anxious. Behind them, in the
distance, was a dark, funnel-shaped cloud.

"Oh, it's a top!" said Belle as it came closer.

She and Blue began to spin it and play with
it just as anyone would spin a small wooden top.
They spun it so hard that it finally broke apart.
As it turns out, it was not a top but a tornado. It
flew away into little puffs of wind, and everyone
in Kansas calmed right down again.

Next, they went west to the Rocky Mountains. These behemoths were just gentle sloping hills to the ox family. They all scampered up the rocky peaks and took turns sliding down the sides of the mountains at high speeds.

Every time they slid down a mountain, the oxen tumbled into the riverbed below. Each time this happened, the riverbed broke open a little more until, finally, Babe landed hard on one spot. The riverbed cracked wide open, leaving high craggy walls and a big path for the Colorado River to rush through. It had been a shallow riverbed before the oxen got there, but they made it into a *Grand* Canyon!

Now it was time to warm up again, so the family headed to southern California. One morning, Belle felt the ground rumbling, and she woke the others up. They all declared that it did indeed feel like the ground was shaking. The family looked outside and found a spot nearby where the Earth seemed to be moving in different directions.

"Well, here's the problem," said Babe. "Let's see if we can fix this."

Babe and Belle stood on one side, and Blue and Bessie stood on the other. They pushed the ground right back together, and the rumbling and shaking suddenly just stopped. That was the end of that earthquake!

Next, they took a swim in the ocean until they ran into the islands of Hawaii. The friendly people gave them flower necklaces which, the oxen family all agreed, made them look quite charming.

One day, Blue and Belle were building a sand castle with very tall towers. All of a sudden, one of Blue's horns banged into one of the towers, knocking the sand castle over. The sand from their castle poured into a hole in one of the mountains, and it cooled down the lava that had been bubbling below. The oxen had stopped the lava flow and put the volcano back to sleep for a thousand more years!

The oxen swam back to the mainland. They trotted their way across deserts, mountains, prairies, cornfields, and rivers. Finally, they reached the Bunyan farm in Minnesota.

The tired oxen family settled down in their beds of straw. The door to the barn was cracked open so that they could see the night sky. They had seen many things and been many places, but they all agreed the stars hanging over the land they knew so well were indeed the finest things they had ever seen.

Think Critically

1. What does the author mean by, "It felt like the sun had come down from the sky and was sitting on the beach"?

2. Why weren't Blue and Belle scared of the tornado?

3. How do you think people felt when they saw the huge oxen?

4. What effect did the Ox family have in New York City?

5. Do you believe anything in this story could really happen? Why or why not?

 Social Studies

Babe's Family Trip Look in an atlas for a map of the United States, including Hawaii. Starting in Minnesota, find all the places the oxen family visited. Estimate how far they traveled to get from one place to the next.

School-Home Connection Share with family members some of the things that were larger than life, or exaggerated, in the story. Then make up some larger than life sentences.

Word Count: 1,226